My name is Lucy Doherty

Helen Santos

By the same author:
Pepe's Dog

© Helen Santos 2003

First published 2003

ISBN 1 85999 744 9

Scripture Union, 207–209 Queensway, Bletchley, Milton Keynes, MK2 2EB, United Kingdom

Email: info@scriptureunion.org.uk
Website: www.scriptureunion.org.uk

Scripture Union Australia, Locked Bag 2, Central Coast Business Centre, NSW 2252, Australia
Website: www.su.org.au

Scripture Union USA, P.O. Box 987, Valley Forge, PA 19482, USA
Website: www.scriptureunion.org

British Library Cataloguing-in-Publication Data.

A catalogue record of this book is available from the British Library.

Printed and bound in Great Britain by Creative Print and Design (Wales) Ebbw Vale.

Cover design: Paul Airy

Scripture Union is an international Christian charity working with churches in more than 130 countries, providing resources to bring the good news about Jesus Christ to children, young people and families and to encourage them to develop spiritually through the Bible and prayer.

As well as our network of volunteers, staff and associates who run holidays, church-based events and school Christian groups, we produce a wide range of publications and support those who use our resources through training programmes.

Name

Subject

Chapter one

My name is Lucy Doherty and this is my first book. I only decided this afternoon that I'm going to be a writer so I don't know yet what my book is going to be about.

We are having a Book Week at school and an author came to talk to our class. She was fun. She told us all about writing and said to put up our hands if we wanted to be authors too. Me and my friend Lottie put our hands up. (I think Lottie only did it for a laugh. She hates anything that means work! Writing a book is work – that's what the author said.)

She also said that one of the best ways to start a book was with a conversation – or a really exciting happening. Wham! You've got to grab your reader from the first moment, or they won't turn over to page 2. She also said you had to write for an imaginary reader – like you are talking to them.

She said that years ago, some authors actually used to call their imaginary reader "dear Reader" and nobody seemed to mind or find it odd. So, dear Reader – whoever you are – I hope you have turned to page 2 because I now have some riveting conversation for you. And it really happened because I have decided that this is going to be a true story and it's going to be the story of my life.

Here comes the conversation. I hope you're hanging on to your seat...

It was when I came home from school and Mum was in the living room. She was bashing away with the iron as usual and watching a chat show on TV. She was doing Samantha Something's ironing – *she* pays £5 an hour so Mum likes to do her ironing. (I call her Samantha Something because her real name is foreign and I can't even say it, let alone spell it and – anyway – Mum calls her Samantha Something too.)

CONVERSATION
Me: Mum.
Mum: Yes, m'darling.
Me: I'm going to write a book.
Mum: Are you, m'darling?
Me: Can I have some money to buy some writing paper?
Mum: There's some writing paper in the drawer.
Me: But I want a proper writing book, to keep it all together. It's going to be a real book.
Mum: Is it, m'darling?
Me: Can I have some money?
Mum: How much do you want?
Me: About a pound.
Mum: A pound is it? For a writing pad! And what have you done with your pocket money?
Me: I didn't know I was going to be a writer or I would have saved some.

Well, I'll stop there because it isn't a very exciting conversation and it's taking up too much space. But it's the sort of conversation me and Mum are always having. She's usually ironing or sewing or cooking because that's how she makes her money, doing things nobody else wants to do. No one knows how to mend clothes these days, but she doesn't mind. She does it for them and watches TV at the same time.

She tells me about some of the people she cleans for but, except for Madame Stravinsky (that's not her real name but that's what Mum calls her), they don't have very exciting lives.

As this book is going to be the story of my life I had better write down a description of myself. The author this afternoon said descriptions are important. She said there's an old-fashioned writer called Charles Dickens, and he could use up a whole page just describing someone's nose. All I can say is, it must have been a very special nose. Mine is quite an ordinary sort of nose, I think – not too long, not too short, and with two holes for breathing.

Mum reckons I look like her. She has black hair and blue eyes and so do I. She says it's the Irish blood. Lots of Irish people have them. She's called Mary. She said lots of girls in Ireland are called Mary, after the Virgin Mary. When she first told me that, I didn't know what she was talking about, so she had to explain to me all about religion, and then said she didn't believe in it and told me not to, either.

Mum's family all live in Ireland. She told me that she ran away from home and came to live in London and she never wants to go back. Mum is a happy sort of person really. The only thing that upsets her (well, perhaps not the *only* thing, but the main thing) is thinking about her family.

"It's just you and me, m'darling," is one of her favourite sayings, so I don't ask her about the family because I know she doesn't want me to.

"What about my dad?" I once asked. I couldn't help it because I was bursting to know.

"Oh, he was a wild one," she said, with a funny kind of look on her face when she said it. It made me think she still liked him – but then she quickly said, "Maybe one day I'll tell you."

I'm really looking forward to that 'one day'. I sometimes make up stories about my dad in my head. I try to imagine what it means to be a wild one. I don't think it means bad. In my dreams he's very handsome – with lots of black curls (like mine) and he's always got a twinkle in his eyes and shining white teeth. And he does Riverdancing like the man on telly. Mum loves watching him.

There's a man in the corner shop who makes me think of my dad. That's why I never mind going there when Mum asks me – but I'd never tell her. She thinks I don't think about him at all, but I do – lots. One day – perhaps when I'm grown up – I'm going to meet him.

The only other person who knows about my dad is Lottie. She lives in the flat upstairs from us and we've been going to the same school since we were in Reception class. For almost as long as I can remember, me and Lottie have been best friends.

Lottie doesn't have a dad either but she says she's glad she hasn't got one because her dad wasn't very nice. She can hardly remember him – only that her mum used to cry a lot when he was around, so they were all very happy when he went away and didn't come back. I'm glad my dad wasn't like that. I don't know why he doesn't live with us, but at least I'm sure he was nice.

Lottie has two little brothers, Franco and Tony. Her real name is Carlotta – her dad was from Italy, which is why they have Italian names. Her mum's English and she and my mum are quite good friends.

Well, I have done so much writing tonight that

Mum thinks I've gone mad. I'm going to bed now and I'm going to think over the story of my life and decide what to write tomorrow.

Oh, I forgot to say that I've just had my eleventh birthday. Mum says that when I was born, I had lots of jet black hair, just like now, and that I was as beautiful as the Queen of Sheba. Who's she? Mum doesn't know either but she must have been famous for her beauty because everybody said it.

Today I asked Lottie if she'd started writing her book. She said, "What book?" She'd forgotten all about it as I knew she would. I told her I'd started mine and had written lots and lots.

"Can I read it?" she said.

I said yes but now I wish I hadn't. It's funny, I don't know why, but all of a sudden I want to keep it secret till it's finished. I have a feeling that if I let anyone see it before it's finished – even Lottie, my best friend – I won't finish it.

Last night Mum said, "Are you going to let me see all this scribbling you're doing, m'darling?" (She always calls me "m'darling". It's like her name for me. She hardly ever calls me Lucy, except when she's mad.) I said, "I expect so. One day." But I don't really want her to see it either. I'll have to find a place to hide it so she won't be able to sneak a look. Not that Mum is a reader. She likes telly too much and, anyway, she says you can't read and do other things at the same time – like ironing or sewing. Which is true.

Lottie doesn't read much either, but she likes to

be read to. I love reading. Lottie and I sit on the stairs and I read to her. Sometimes Franco and Tony come and listen, too, but not when it's a girlie story. Only when it's adventures. I told Mum I could read to her while she's doing things and sometimes she lets me, but only when it doesn't mean her missing something special on TV. She's really hooked!

I suppose there's worse things to be hooked on – like DRUGS. Greg downstairs has that problem. He used to be quite nice. Lottie and I both fancied him once but now he's thin and dirty and twitches all the time and we're a bit scared of him. Mum says she feels sorry for his mum, who always did her best for him. She's going round the bend, Mum says, and I think it's true. Sometimes we hear them shouting at each other.

Mum says, "Let it be a lesson to you. Never take drugs."

Name _____

Subject _____

_____

Chapter two

I didn't write a lot yesterday because EXCITING THINGS happened after tea. Lottie and I spent most of the time watching. Some new people have moved into the ground-floor flat that's been empty for ages. We knew somebody was going to come soon because some men from the council came and took down all the boards from the windows and chucked out all the old muck and junk. And yesterday, just after tea, Lottie rang the bell and asked if I wanted to come and watch.

A big van had just arrived and we decided it would be fun to find out what was in it and see what the new people were like. It's a three-bedroom flat like Lottie's so they must have children.

Mum said I could go down with Lottie but that I shouldn't get in the way. She was going to watch from the window. So we sat on the wall right by the van and watched all the boxes and bits of furniture going in. It's funny to think you can put a whole house in a van. How can there be room?

The new people were helping to carry in some of the bits the men were putting on the pavement. Franco asked if he could help carry something and they said yes. Soon we were all carrying something – I carried a pink lampshade into the flat. Mum would have called it 'getting in the way' and it did get a bit crowded at times. I don't think the men from the van were very pleased. Then the lady said we could all come in the kitchen and have some squash and biscuits as soon as we could find the box they were in.

Suddenly we were running all over the place, looking in all the boxes. There seemed to be loads of us – not just me and Lottie and her brothers.

Some of the other kids are right little thieves – I hope nothing got stolen. If it did, I hope they won't think it was us.

At last we found the right box. She (the lady I mean, I don't know her name yet) said it was her 'Club Box'. It was fun standing in the kitchen with boxes and black plastic bags all round and drinking squash together as if we were all the best of friends (which we AREN'T because some of the kids there we just wouldn't be seen dead with normally).

Franco said, "Why do you call it your Club Box?" and she said, "Because we had a kids' club where we lived before and we got through lots of squash and biscuits."

"What kind of club?" asked Franco. You could never call Franco shy. Lottie's mum says he's an embarrassment and she sometimes has to pretend he doesn't belong to her. But he's quite nice really – sometimes.

"Well, we called it 'Explorers'," said the lady. "We were trying to find out about God."

One of the boys said a rude word and everyone laughed (well, not everyone). Franco still wasn't put off. "Are you going to have a club here?" he said. Lottie pushed him hard and whispered, "Shut up." You could see she was embarrassed but that made it worse. "Why should I shut up?" he complained as loud as possible. "Why can't I ask?"

The lady didn't seem to mind. "We'll have to wait and see," she said. "Would you like us to?"

"Don't know," said Franco and after that we all left. We'd had our biscuits and squash and there wasn't really anything else to do. Lottie and I sat on the stairs outside her flat for a while. We decided the new people seemed all right but we still didn't know if they had any children. We hadn't seen any but, as Lottie said, you can't get a three-bedroom council flat if you haven't got kids.

Lottie and I like sitting on the stairs. It's our special place. Lottie's mum likes to keep everything neat and tidy, and doesn't want kids coming in to play. My mum isn't all that tidy but she's always got lots of other people's ironing and sewing all over the place so she isn't keen on me bringing friends in – in case they mess up the piles or even pinch something. She knows Lottie's OK and sometimes she comes into my bedroom, but mostly we sit on the stairs. Lottie lives in the top flat, so we don't get in the way.

When we were little we used to play games on the stairs, like jumping, or dolls, and the different steps were different rooms. But we haven't done that for a while now. I suppose we're growing up. Now we look at magazines together and talk about our fave pop stars.

∧∧∧∧∧∧∧∧∧∧

I've been thinking about the new people and their Explorer Club. And finding out about God. I'd quite like to find out about God. It's no good asking Mum. She says it's all rubbish and I know she doesn't like talking about it. Religion causes wars, she says.

At school we have to learn things about God. The trouble is, there seem to be so many different gods and some of them don't like it if you eat certain foods or don't dress in special ways. And everybody has a different day for worshipping their god (perhaps so as not to fight about it). I wonder what you do when you worship? Is it like the feeling I get when I look at pictures of – (I'm not telling you who he is) – or when I sometimes think about my dad?

It's hard to describe feelings or understand them. Some feelings are nice, like when me and Lottie get all excited about a book I'm reading to her. I hate feeling scared. I feel scared if I go shopping for Mum and I think the Kelly boys might stop me and try to get the money off me. They did that once and said if I told Mum what had happened they'd beat me up so I never told her. I said I'd lost it and she was angry.

"Think of all the ironing I had to do for that fiver!" she said. And I felt angry too, and I hate those boys. Sometimes I wish there was a god who would pay them back for all the nasty things they do and get away with because everyone's scared of them.

But that's not the only reason why I wish there was a god. Sometimes I feel lonely. I know I've got Mum and I've got Lottie and they're my very best friends (Mum first, of course), but I can't tell them everything. I think if God existed I could tell him everything.

Sometimes I do talk to him. I say, "God, if you're there, why can't you make my dad come home and want to know me? Why did you let old Mrs Greenaway's dog get run over when she loved it so much and it was all she had, and her husband had only just died?" Mum told me she'd been so upset on the day of the funeral that she must have left the door open. Little Binky went to look for her and got squashed by a bus.

I once asked the RE teacher which god was the real one, or the most important one, and she said she couldn't answer that question. I'd have to find out for myself. Her job was to tell us about them all and I'd better ask my mum if I wanted to know more. I told her, "My mum says it's all rubbish," and I don't think she liked that. "Well, you've still got to study the subject," she said in a huff. I didn't mean to upset her. I was only telling her what Mum thinks.

Perhaps I can get to know the new people a bit better and find out about their club.

Last Saturday me and Lottie rang their bell. We were on our way to the corner shop for our mums and decided we'd ask the lady there if she wanted anything. A girl about the same age as us answered the door. She was pale and thin and looked a bit stuck up. This wasn't a good start. We didn't know what to say. We just stared at each other and then Lottie started giggling. She's always giggling. She's as bad as Franco with his questions.

I put on my posh voice. "Is your mother at home?" I said and this made Lottie burst into laughter. I was beginning to get mad at her and at this girl who just stared at us like we were aliens from Mars.

"Mum," she shouted. (Only she didn't really shout. She sort of called, a bit like grown-ups do.) "It's two girls want to see you."

"Tell them to come in then."

The lady was in the kitchen and she popped her head out. She remembered us straight away and gave us a big smile. "Oh, hello. You're the girls from upstairs. You helped with the moving. This is my daughter Ruth."

"We're just going shopping and wondered if we could bring you anything," I managed to say, suddenly feeling a bit shy and silly.

"What a lovely thought. I tell you what, though. Why not take Ruth with you and show her where the shops are. Then when you come back we can all get to know each other better. We're still in a terrible muddle and the boys haven't woken up yet. They only arrived last night."

She gave Ruth some money for bread and milk and off we all went together. Lottie was still giggling, Ruth was still silent and I was wishing I'd never thought of the idea. We saw the Kelly boys and had to make a detour round the back of the flats before they saw us. By the time we'd done that and explained why, we'd got talking and Ruth didn't seem stuck up or shy any more. She said she'd be starting school after the half-term holiday and she's probably going to be in our class. 'The boys' are three-year-old twins, Simon and Andrew.

When we went back we met their dad – properly, I mean. We'd seen him when they were moving in, but he'd been too busy to talk to us. He's a bit fat and half bald, but his eyes are smiley and he's very friendly. Lottie and I aren't used to dads so we didn't know what to say to him. They asked if we wanted some breakfast with them – it was 10.30 and they still hadn't had breakfast, but we said no.

We met the twins who looked like clones with runny noses. Lottie oohed and aahed over them because she loves little kids. Maybe because she's got brothers. I'm used to being on my own so I didn't know what to say to them. They just stared at me with their big grey eyes, but they soon started showing Lottie their favourite toys.

I didn't want to ask about the Explorers Club in front of Lottie just in case she thought I was mad. Ruth came later and sat with us on the stairs and we told her all about school and the different people who live in the flats.

Ruth has a pet Russian hamster called Chico. She had him in her pocket and he is so little and grey. He's really cute! At school we've got ordinary golden hamsters. I'd never seen a Russian one before. "He bites," she said. Lottie didn't believe her and got bitten.

Her finger started to bleed. Me and Ruth laughed but Lottie started to cry and went home. I felt a bit mean, sitting just the other side of her door, knowing she was crying, but Lottie does get into a huff sometimes and doesn't want to talk to me. Mum says it's her Italian blood but I don't know what that has to do with it.

Name

Subject

Chapter three

I've been so busy that I haven't written my book for ages. In fact, I'd forgotten all about it until Mum said, "What about your book? Have you finished it? Can I read it?"

I told her I'd got stuck. I didn't want to tell her the truth because she's always telling me I get bored of things.

"Can I help you get unstuck?" she said. For a change, she wasn't actually doing anything, except having a cup of tea and dunking a biscuit. Fortunately, the biscuit plopped into the tea and she got busy trying to fish it out with her spoon. This gave me time to think of an excuse because I don't want her to know what I'm writing, especially the bits about my dad.

"No, I know what to do now," I said – and it was sort of true. The author said that when you get stuck, change the subject or bring in a new character, or make something unexpected happen, something you hadn't thought of before.

Well, I've already brought in a new character – Ruth – and as this is a true story I don't want to invent someone. It's funny. When I first met Ruth, I didn't think I was going to like her. I thought she was a bit of a snob. But she isn't really, just a bit shy. The teacher let her sit with me and Lottie when school started so, apart from always being together at school, we also hang around together after school. Ruth's mum doesn't mind her inviting friends in and, as it's getting a bit cold to sit on the stairs, we go to her flat instead.

Ruth is a brilliant friend. She has lots of books and doesn't mind me borrowing them. We talk about books all the time because she likes reading the same as me. We shut the bedroom door to keep the twins out and it's cosy and warm in there. Her parents haven't had time to decorate her room yet but somehow you don't notice the grotty walls. We sit on her bed with the duvet over us and talk and talk.

The trouble is, Lottie doesn't like it. She says I'm supposed to be *her* best friend, not Ruth's. I said I could be best friends with both of them but Lottie says you can't have two best friends. So now she's in a huff. It's not as bad as it might be, because Lottie loves playing with the twins. So we both go to Ruth's but she doesn't come in the bedroom. We said she could but she said there wasn't room for three.

She's now hanging around with another girl at school – Tracey Bignall. I know she's only doing it to annoy me. TB hates me – she's always being rude about Irish people – and she makes Lottie laugh a lot. Lottie's always laughing, but now I think they are laughing at me and Ruth.

Yesterday we had a BIG row, me and Lottie. TB banged into Ruth in the corridor on purpose and made her hit her head against the wall. Lottie laughed and that made me really angry because I knew Ruth was trying hard not to cry.

"Shove her back," I said.

"She's too scared," shouted TB, so I shoved her instead and sent her flying. She didn't exactly fall over but she looked quite stupid trying to keep her balance. Her face went bright red. She looked like she was going to hit someone and I thought I was in big trouble. Ruth's face was white as a piece of new paper and suddenly she was sick all over the floor.

I was safe because TB could only hit me by treading in it, which she didn't want to do. So she and Lottie went running off and me and Ruth stayed in the corridor. Ruth was all shivery. A teacher turned up, and they phoned Ruth's mum and she came and took her home.

I told Lottie she couldn't be both my friend and TB's and she said I couldn't be both her friend and Ruth's. "Ruth's not mean like TB," I said, "and you shouldn't have laughed when she was hurt."

"Ruth, Ruth, Ruth. That's all you talk about!" Lottie shouted and there were tears in her eyes. And then she went in and slammed the door in my face.

I don't like rows, especially with Lottie, and now I don't know what to do. This book is getting exciting, but it's not the kind of exciting I like. It's horrible. I wish I could talk to Mum but she's glued to the telly as usual. I think I'll just go to bed. I'll think about my dad and pretend he's coming on Saturday to take me somewhere, like some dads do. I'll think of all the places we might go to. He'll give me a choice of three places and I'll have to make up my mind. I often do that. It's fun. And I usually fall asleep in the middle. Goodnight, dear Reader.

∧∧∧∧∧∧∧∧

Because of writing about the BIG ROW I didn't have time to say anything about the two other things that have happened. One was the flat warming at Ruth's and the other was going to church for the very first time.

Only a week after Ruth's family (the Prices) moved in, they sent printed invitations to everyone in the flats inviting us to their 'Flat Warming'. You could tell it was done on a computer because it had party pictures on it – balloons, confetti and little people with laughing faces. It was printed in different colours too. It said:

"The Prices have just moved in and we'd like to get to know all our new neighbours and hope you'd like to get to know us. So it's open house at 16A from 11 am to 4 pm this Saturday. Drop in any time and say hello. Tea, coffee, light snacks on tap."

I'm going to keep the invitation with this book.

"I wonder if they've invited everyone?" Mum asked Lottie's mum. They agreed they'd go together in the morning. I like to listen when our mums are chatting together. They forget I'm there and sometimes I hear all sorts of things I'm not supposed to know.

"Well, they'd better watch out if the Kelly family turns up. They'll go through the place like a dose of salts," said Lottie's mum.

My mum agreed and said someone should warn them about the Kellys. I heard her telling Mrs Price all about their thieving ways and how Mr Kelly was always in trouble with the police.

To tell the truth, when you look round Ruth's home there's not much worth pinching. Two long settees in the living room take up most of the space. Their telly is in the kitchen, on a special shelf on the wall. It's only a little one. Ruth has told me they don't watch telly much.

The place soon got crowded at the flat warming, mostly with women and kids. Lottie went off with the twins to their bedroom. Tony and Franco soon got bored, but Mr Price put a video on in the kitchen. Most of the kids watched it while their mums yabbered in the living room. Ruth and I helped her mum dish up drinks for the kids.

The most the Kellys did when they came was stuff themselves with crisps and peanuts and wander around like hungry dogs. Mr Price got talking to them. They were really rude and cheeky with him at first but he didn't seem to mind and later I saw they were getting on all right and he was showing them some photos.

Later, Lottie and I saw the photos too. It was a summer camp with swimming and canoeing and abseiling and all that sort of stuff. It looked really fun and me and Lottie said we'd like to go there one day. We've never done anything like that before.

"Well, if you save up your pocket money it might be possible," said Mr Price. His name is Jeff, but Mum says it isn't polite to call grown-ups by their first names. I told her he said I could but she said not to. So I don't know what to do about that. My mum's dead old-fashioned at times.

Afterwards she said she thought they were all right, but that she didn't want to be friends with religious people.

"Are they religious?" I asked. I didn't know what she meant.

"Well, they told me they'd moved here to get involved with the church down the road, so they must be. They'll be trying to convert us next."

"What does that mean?" I asked.

"Oh, making us believe in God and go to church and everything."

"Is that bad?" I wondered, because I'd never really thought about it.

"It's a waste of time."

"Could I go if I wanted to?"

"Have they been getting at you already?" she demanded suspiciously. "Are they only making friends with you for that?"

I felt uncomfortable. I didn't know what to say.

"It's only that Ruth said I could come to Sunday Club with her if I wanted to. I never do anything on Sundays anyway and it might be fun. Ruth says it's fun. It's only for an hour or so. And I'm sure she'd still be my friend even if I said no."

Mum stared at me. I could see she didn't know what to say.

"Please," I begged. "I promise I won't go again if it's bad or horrible or something. It's just that Ruth said I'd like it and she's my friend."

"And what about Lottie?"

"Well, Lottie can come too if she wants to, if her mum lets her."

Lottie's mum wouldn't let her. She said they had a different religion so she couldn't go to the church up the road. It didn't matter that Lottie reminded her mum that they never went anywhere to church anyway. She just said she couldn't go and that was that. By this time, I'd persuaded Mum to say yes, as long as I didn't come home talking about God and things, and Lottie was upset and said it wasn't fair. It was one of the things that led to the BIG ROW.

She said I was always doing things with Ruth now instead of with her and that if I really *was* her friend I'd stay with her on Sunday instead of going off with Ruth.

I said it wasn't my fault her mum wouldn't let her go to Sunday Club and why should I stop doing something I wanted to do just cos she couldn't do it with me. Anyway, I've already written about the BIG ROW so I won't go on about it. Tomorrow I'll write about church as I'm tired now. My wrist is aching. Being a writer is hard work!

Name

Subject

Chapter four

It's funny how you can go past places nearly every day and never even notice them. The church Ruth took me to is just down the road and we go past it on our way to school, but I never wondered what it was. I suppose I never really saw it. It's a great big building made of grey-brown bricks. There are lots of huge trees which hide the front of it – maybe that's why I never noticed.

The branches hang over the pavement and in autumn the leaves are thick on the ground. When I was little I used to love swishing through them but now I don't bother. In fact, once I slipped over on them on a wet day and Mum said they ought to clean the leaves up instead of leaving them for people to have accidents on.

The leaves hide puddles, too. When we went on Sunday the twins splashed into one – quite a deep one – so before they got into church their feet were really wet. They didn't seem to mind, though. Mrs Price was worried they'd catch cold, but Mr Price (Jeff) said wet feet never hurt anyone.

I was a bit scared about going into church. I'm not sure why. Maybe because Mum didn't really want me to go but had made me dress up anyway.

"You can't go to church in jeans and a T-shirt," she said.

"Why not?"

"Because you can't. You have to dress properly."

"Did you have to dress properly when you went to church?" I asked. I thought it might be a good chance to find out why Mum is so against it.

"To be sure I did. Nobody would dream of going any other way. Now, make sure you don't get brainwashed," she warned me as I went out of the door to meet Ruth.

I'm not quite sure what brainwashing means. How can you wash your brains? Yuck! But I promised, anyway, and told Jeff (Mr P), and he promised he'd make sure it didn't happen to me.

Ruth and I started discussing how you wash brains and whether they'd be slippery or quite easy to hold. In the end, Mrs P said it means being told what to think and not being allowed to think for yourself. That sounded pretty boring and the sort of thing we do at school.

My hand is getting tired so I don't want to do lots of writing. Perhaps I might be a poet. Poems are much shorter than books. And descriptions are so difficult! I've been just sitting for a while, thinking about church. I'd rather not describe it but if I'm going to be a real writer I'll have to try. I think I'll just put down what comes into my head.

The church was so big – the main part, anyway. There was a sort of hall where you first go in with blue carpet on the floor and pictures on the walls. We had drinks and biscuits there afterwards and everybody hung around talking. That part was bright and sort of cosy. They had display boards with letters and photos. Ruth said she thought the letters were from people who go to other countries to tell other people about God.

First we had to go into the main part of the church and that was E-NOR-MOUS! Although there were lots of lights, it was still a bit dark, except at the front. There it was full of light and there was a table with enormous candles at each end on a beautiful white cloth with embroidery all round the edges. In the middle was a cross that shone like silver and there were lovely flowers to one side. I couldn't stop looking and I forgot that the rest was so dark because all the time we were looking at the cross and the candles. It was magic. The ceiling seemed a long way off but it had lovely patterns on it.

There was a man with a long black dress (though I could see he was wearing trousers underneath) with a white robe over it. Ruth told me his name was David and that he's the vicar. "What's a vicar?" I asked.

"I don't know," she said, "but that's what he is. It means he's in charge."

There were lots of kids and we all had to sit in the front rows. Some, like me and Ruth, were very quiet but some were fidgety all the time. We had to sing some songs and listen to some talking and then we went off to the Sunday Club. Jeff was in charge of our group, with a helper called Vicky – it was great.

Jeff's really clever. He plays the guitar and knows how to make us laugh. We talked about Christmas. It's ages away yet but Jeff said, "I bet some of you are wondering what you're going to get for Christmas. It takes ages to get ready, saving money, deciding what presents to buy, when to put up the tree, wondering whether to invite Uncle Kevin again after he pinched all the best bits of turkey for himself last year."

I can't remember everything we talked about, but Jeff said it took God a long time to get ready for Christmas, too, and had we thought about that? He said we'd talk about that next week and now I'm wondering how God got ready for Christmas.

I'd love to ask Mum if she knows but I daren't. I've promised not to. But I'm really looking forward to going again.

Dear Reader, have you ever made toffee? I have. Ruth and I made it for the very first time the other day. It was her idea. She came to spend the night with me because Madame Stravinsky was having one of her 'Chez Moi's. That's a French way of saying 'At my place'. I only know how to spell it because we've started doing a bit of French at school.

Mum says Madame S likes using French words for things. She works for television, but she's not an actress or anything like that. She produces things. "Rabbits out of a hat, I shouldn't wonder," Mum said when I asked what she produced. I don't think she knows really. She's one of those people whose name comes up at the end of a programme in little letters that no one reads.

She doesn't know how to do ordinary things but she's very important and earns oodles of money. She lives in a beautiful house just round the corner from here. I love walking down her road. Everyone who lives there must be rich. But Mum says she's North Five the same as we are, whatever that means.

Mum puts up with her because she gives her rush jobs, sewing and ironing, and doesn't mind how much she pays, and when she has her 'Chez Moi's – in other words, a party – she asks Mum to be like a waitress. She has to serve food and drinks and do the washing up and she doesn't get home till early in the morning. So I asked if Ruth could spend the night because I hate being on my own.

"Not Lottie?" asked Mum, because it's always been Lottie before.

I held my breath. Mum doesn't know me and Lottie have fallen out and I don't want her to.

"Just for a change," I said. "I'm always at Ruth's."

And then I breathed out because Mum just said OK, as long as Mrs Price didn't mind popping up from time to time to keep an eye on us. So Ruth came. We watched a cookery programme on TV and Ruth said she'd once made toffee with her mum. That's the only cooking she'd ever done and it was really easy.

"Why don't we make some now?" I suggested. I was inspired by the programme to have a go. I only ever cook stuff like beans on toast.

"It depends if you've got the right ingredients."

So we looked in the cupboards. There was plenty of sugar and butter, Irish butter. "The best," Mum says. "None of the pretend stuff for us, m'darling."

"We also need some vinegar," said Ruth.

"Vinegar!" I exclaimed. "Yuck. Vinegar toffee!" But she said the stuff she'd made with her mum had vinegar in it. Luckily, we had vinegar too because Mum often brings supper from the chippie and they're stingy with the vinegar, so we've got a big bottle of our own.

Ruth said that all we had to do was let it boil in a pan until it was ready. It was good fun making it. Ruth wanted to be in charge because she'd done it before and could show me. But I reminded her that we were in my kitchen using my stuff.

"It's not yours, it's your mum's," she said.

"All the more reason for me doing it," I said. "She'll blame me if anything goes wrong."

"Do you think she'll mind us cooking?" asked Ruth seriously. "We haven't asked permission."

"She hasn't said we can't," I said, rather cleverly I thought.

"Because she didn't know we were going to." Ruth looked happy, as if she'd proved I was wrong.

"Well, my mum's always saying what the eye doesn't see the heart doesn't grieve over," I told her.

"Yes, but…"

I could see Ruth was getting all mixed up about it. That's one of the bad things about going to church. You get too worried about what's right and wrong. After all, what could possibly be wrong about making a bit of toffee?

"Perhaps we could go down to my flat and make it," said Ruth half-heartedly, but we didn't and we soon had the sugar and butter and vinegar boiling away on the cooker and we didn't burn ourselves or set the house on fire or anything.

We had to pour it into a sponge tin, only we weren't quite sure when. Ruth said it would get hard quite quickly – as soon as it was cold – but we waited for ages and ages and it never did. It still tasted good, though. It was all chewy and runny and yummy. We sat at the kitchen table with a teaspoon each and ate it all up without thinking, while nattering about fave pop stars, fave food and fave boys (not many of them!). Most of the boys at school are yuck.

Ruth suddenly said, "We should have saved some

for Lottie."

I said, "Why?"

"Because it would show her we wanted to be friends again."

"She's the one who doesn't want to be friends," I said. "I haven't done anything wrong."

Ruth was silent for a while. I wasn't sure if it was because her teeth were stuck together with toffee – she was wriggling a finger in her mouth like me – or whether she was thinking. Maybe it was both.

"Perhaps if we just said sorry," she suggested. With almost a flash of my Irish temper I answered, "Sorry for what?" Which scared her a lot, I think.

(I don't know if Irish tempers are different to other people's, and if they are I can't help it, being Irish, I mean. Mum says Lottie has an Italian temper – sort of smouldering – and if smouldering means going on quietly for a long time, she's right. I just flare up, but then I'm all right afterwards. Mostly I can't even remember what I was cross about. Mum's like that, too.)

"Well, just sorry that we aren't all friends any more."

"She started it," I said.

Ruth was looking uncomfortable. Her face went a bit pink as she went on, "Jesus says we ought to forgive people."

"*They* ought to say sorry first, then. I *will* forgive her if *she* says sorry."

This time Ruth's face went absolutely scarlet. "I think he wants us to forgive people even when they don't say sorry."

"Even when they've been really horrible?"

Ruth nodded without looking at me. She could

see I didn't like what she was saying. When she's too serious, that's when I'd rather be with Lottie. She doesn't go on at me and try to turn me into a goody-goody like Ruth does.

Just then, Ruth's mum rang the bell. She wanted to remind us about going to bed. By the time she'd done that and chatted with us for a while, everything was OK again. We started talking about books and didn't go to bed until midnight.

Next day, Mum was mad because we'd left the saucepan in a mess and she couldn't get the dried bits of toffee out of it. It had gone hard! And we'd used all the butter so she couldn't have any on her toast.

Ruth has been away all Christmas. She's staying with an auntie in Hastings, by the sea. She says maybe one day I can go with her. There's a castle as well as the seaside. I'd love to visit a castle – and the seaside. Mum said she took me when I was little and I was so scared of the waves she never took me again. There's a photo of me looking miserable on a stony beach somewhere when I was about two, but I can't remember it.

When I said I didn't think I'd be scared of the waves now, Mum just said, "And what's so special about the sea anyway? It's so wet and all!" She says funny things sometimes, probably because she's not really thinking. She's usually watching telly when we talk. We had a brand new telly for Christmas, twice as big as the one before. Still the same programmes though.

Ruth gave me a bookmark for Christmas, with words done in cross stitch. "God is good." Her mum and dad gave me a Bible to put it in. Mum sort of sniffed when she saw the Bible but all she said was, "That'll keep you busy for a while. Give me *EastEnders* any day."

I had to go to Lottie's at Christmas cos our mums always like to get together. Before it used to be fun, one of the few times when me and Lottie could get together in her room, but we didn't do that this time. We just sat on her posh sofa and watched a video while our mums nattered. It was awful, my very worst Christmas so far, especially when Mum started nagging me when we got home – as if it was my fault!

I didn't want to tell Mum how horrible Lottie is being to me and Ruth so I just kept quiet and in the end Mum said, "Ah well, it's a phase you're going through. I dare say you'll be thick as thieves again by the spring."

I hate it when Mum talks about phases. I'm not a little kid any more and I don't have phases. But if I say that she just laughs and says that me getting mad just proves her point. You can't win when you've got a mum like mine. Still, she did let me choose my own clothes for Christmas AND paid more than she said she would. I'm dying to show them to Ruth when she gets back. Tomorrow, I think.

Mum's quite happy about me being friends with Ruth and has got used to me going to church on Sundays. We had a special carol service and were supposed to invite our family and friends but I didn't say anything to Mum and there wasn't any point in asking Lottie. So I just went with Ruth's family and it was lovely.

We were all given an orange with a little candle stuck in it to remind us that Jesus is the light of the world, and I sat and looked at my candle flame, which burned bright on the shelf where we put our hymn books, and felt all warm and special inside. Then Winston, who is a right pain in the neck, blew it out. Ruth lit it again from her candle and I stuck my tongue out at Winston. He only laughed.

We buried Ruth's hamster Chico the other day, and that made me feel sad. He got out of his cage and nobody noticed until Ruth's dad accidentally stepped on him and squashed him. He was only a little hamster, and her dad has big feet. He was wearing his boots, too, because he'd been up the park playing football with us till it got dark.

Ruth wanted a proper funeral for him so we buried him in the window box on our little balcony. (The ground outside was too hard, it being January and she hasn't got any window boxes.) And she said at funerals you say, "Dust to dust, ashes to ashes," because she'd seen it in a film on TV. And that's because when God first made people the Bible says he made them out of dust and we go back to being dust when we die. We both cried a bit, me because I felt sad for Ruth as well as for Chico, and then when we'd finished covering up his little body (she'd wrapped him in a Christmas hanky) I couldn't help wondering what happened next, I mean after you're dead.

"What about heaven?" I said, because I don't fancy just being a bit of dust one day.

"Oh, it's only your body that goes back to dust," she said. "You go to heaven, at least you do if you believe in Jesus."

As I'm not sure whether I believe in Jesus, even though I go to church with her nearly every Sunday, I didn't like to ask any more questions. She goes on a bit when you give her half a chance, all about heaven and hell, and I don't know how to stop her. That's when I miss being friends with Lottie. She was always a laugh and was never serious about anything.

I wish we could be friends again but she has got in with TB's crowd so now we are ENEMIES and she makes fun of me for going to church on Sundays.

She went to Midnight Mass at Christmas. But when I reminded her about that she said, "So what?

That's just a tradition. Like Father Christmas and Christmas trees and things. And I have to go anyway because Mum makes me. You go because you want to. You've gone all goody-goody, just like Ruth."

"I'd rather be goody-goody than go around with TB," I told her, which is true. If Lottie's mum knew who she was with she wouldn't be very pleased.

Name _____

Subject _____

_____
_____*Chapter six*_____

I've been lying on my bed thinking. I had my music on but I wasn't really listening. I was thinking about my dad and God. Jeff was telling us about God being like a dad – a really good dad who doesn't let you down and knows all about you and really loves you.

Jeff's not a bit like I imagine my dad. Sometimes he makes me think of a cuddly bear, especially when he's playing with the twins. He lies on the floor and lets them climb all over him and fight him. He makes all these growly noises and they make growly noises back. It all gets very hectic, and Mrs P has to tell them to stop.

At Sunday Club he's more like a friend than a teacher. He does teach us stuff but it's more like he's just sharing things with us – giving us ideas and expecting us to think them through. I like that. And when he plays the guitar, sometimes he's really funny, jumping about and wriggling like a pop-singer. Not with every song. Not with the serious ones. And he always listens to what you say as if it matters. Even with Winston, although everyone knows that Winston never says anything sensible.

Ruth's dead lucky to have a dad like Jeff. She's really lucky to have a dad.

I started to wonder why my dad has never been to see me. I always tell myself he loves me but how can he love me if he doesn't know me? I don't know him but I love him. At least, I think I do. I dream about meeting him one day and his twinkling eyes making me feel all warm inside, a bit like the man at the shop. I can't say my dad has ever let me down. You can't let someone down if you've never promised them anything, can you?

Jeff said Jesus is the same as God and, if we want him to, he will come and live in our hearts. Winston, who's always trying to be clever, said, "He'd have to be pretty tiny, then." But Jeff said it was a good point. Jesus couldn't really live inside us if he was still a person like he used to be, so he had to find a different way to do it.

"Shrink!" shouted Winston.

"Change," said Jeff.

He sent a different part of himself, called the Holy Spirit, who can live in as many people as he wants to at the same time.

When he was talking about it at Sunday Club I didn't understand, but just now while I've been thinking about my dad, it kind of makes sense. Sometimes I can sort of feel my dad in my heart, as if he belongs to me. He's like a secret in there cos I can't tell Mum. I'd be scared she'd say something that would spoil it all, and he'd disappear and never come back, as if he'd never been there. One day, when I'm grown up, I'm going to look for him. And I just know he'll be pleased to see me.

Jeff said the Holy Spirit was like the wind. You can't see the wind but you know it's there because you can feel it. And in a way you can see it when you see the leaves being blown about. Jeff said Jesus only comes when we ask him to, and when we really mean it. He said that because Winston (as usual) started being stupid and saying, "Here, Jesus, here, boy," like he was calling a dog.

Lottie would have laughed her head off. I wish she would come to Sunday Club with us. When I think of Lottie, I get all cold and angry inside. How could she just stop being my friend? But, as Mum sometimes says about things that go wrong, "It's a closed door, m'darling. Forget it."

My dad is a closed door. I wonder if she's forgotten him? How can I tell? She doesn't know what I think about Dad – or about God – or about anything really important.

And now a horrible thought has just hit me. Was my dad as bad as Lottie's? Is that why Mum never says anything about him? She doesn't want me to know how bad he is. No. It can't be that. I just know it can't though I can't explain why.

If only I dared ask her. Perhaps one day I will.

We met Greg on the stairs yesterday. I'm glad I was with Mum cos I would have been frightened if I'd been on my own. I haven't see him for ages but he looked awful – and a bit mad (Mum said desperate, not mad). He asked Mum for money. He really begged her. He was crying.

And she said, "I'm sorry, m'darling. I'd give it you if it'd do you any good but I know you're only going to buy another nail in your coffin."

He was standing right across the stairs so we couldn't get by, holding the railing with one hand and with the other almost poking Mum in the chest.

"Please," he said. "Please. Just this once."

But she shook her head, grabbed me by the hand and pushed past him. We were delivering some laundry so the big bag helped with the pushing. He didn't stop us, and for a while we just walked in silence until Mum said, "That poor mother of his.

That poor mother."

Seeing Greg like that made the whole morning go sort of grey. I was scared, not so much scared that he'd hurt us, but scared because of what can happen to people.

Mum started saying what a nice boy he used to be and how he'd passed all his GCSEs, and I can just remember how good-looking he was. Lottie and I wrote him a love letter once and pushed it through his letter box. And after that we couldn't stop giggling whenever we saw him (we were only eight then). I bet he thought we were stupid. Once he said, "Here, kids," and gave us some sweets. I wonder if Tony or Franco could end up like Greg one day?

I just HATE, HATE, HATE everyone who sells drugs because of what they've done to Greg. I don't care that Ruth says you shouldn't hate people. Right now I'm almost bursting inside with hate, and I'm scared, too, because grown-ups don't seem to know how to put things right.

∿∿∿∿∿∿∿∿

I've been looking at the Bible that Jeff gave me for Christmas and reading bits of it, too. It's got lots of coloured pictures as well as drawings so it's quite fun to look at. There's a picture of a huge fish opening its mouth to let a tiny man drop in – Jonah. I've heard of him before. I wonder if that story can be true? Seems a bit like a fairy tale to me but I like the idea of someone living inside a fish. It must be really smelly and dark. Would there be room to move about? How would you breathe?

The more I think about it, the more impossible it

seems, but when I asked Ruth and told her what I thought – that it couldn't be true – she almost got huffy and said EVERYTHING in the Bible is absolutely true. It didn't matter if we couldn't understand it. We just had to believe. She thought I was laughing about it and making fun of Jonah. Ruth is just too serious sometimes. If Lottie and I had been talking about Jonah we wouldn't have stopped giggling for ages.

At Sunday Club I asked Jeff if the story about Jonah was true. He said the same as Ruth but that it didn't matter if I couldn't believe it. He said one day, when I know God, I'll be able to believe lots of things I can't believe now. He said once you know God, it's like having a light switched on. There's lots of dark corners we can't see into, but once the light's switched on suddenly we can see and understand things we never could before. He made it sound exciting.

I asked Ruth if her light was switched on and she thought I was laughing at her again. I wasn't but she wouldn't believe me. We nearly fell out, especially because I couldn't help making what I thought were fun remarks, just because she went so serious on me. But she took them the wrong way. She's so stuffy sometimes.

The last picture in the Bible is of a rainbow and people standing underneath it with their arms outstretched. And it says, "And now I make all things new." I suppose it's God saying that – or Jesus. I'm still not sure of the difference between God and Jesus. Jeff says Jesus IS God. I must remember to ask him to explain. Perhaps he has done but I've forgotten.

I'd rather ask Jeff because Ruth sometimes thinks I'm making fun of her when I ask her things about God. I'm not. I know people at school laugh at her, especially TB's gang. She goes all red in the face but at least she has the guts to put up with it. I asked her once why she doesn't just keep quiet. She said, "If you really believe something you have to say so." I don't know if I would.

Till I started going to Sunday Club with Ruth I never bothered with religion – except for homework, which doesn't count. You have to learn about it. But Ruth somehow seems to know about God in a way they don't teach at school. Almost like knowing him as a friend, even somehow loving him.

Mum says, "Keep off religion, m'darling. It causes nothing but trouble." And that seems to be true. People are always hating each other because of religion, and having wars. Maybe Mum's right. Perhaps if I hadn't started going to Sunday Club with Ruth I'd still be friends with Lottie and Lottie wouldn't be mixed up with TB's gang and on the verge of TROUBLE.

Name

Subject

Chapter seven

TB's gang are going round with the Kelly boys and everyone knows what they get up to. I don't know whether to tell Mum but then she might tell Lottie's mum and Lottie would hate me more than ever. On Saturdays they go to the shops and steal whatever's going, just for the fun of it. They don't even want the things they pinch. They just grab whatever's nearest and then show off to see who's pinched the most.

I don't know if Lottie's actually stolen anything yet, but just being with them is bad enough. Suppose they get caught? No one's going to believe she's innocent, even if she is. Ruth and I have been talking about it and we don't know what to do. Ruth said to tell her parents and see what they say, but that seems like sneaking somehow, though her mum and dad are good at sorting things out.

I like the rainbow picture in the Bible and what it says underneath about God making everything new. If it's true he could make things new between me and Lottie. He could make things new for Greg so that he wouldn't want drugs any more.

HE COULD CHANGE THE WHOLE WORLD AND MAKE IT BETTER. So why doesn't he, then? I wish I could understand.

Today at Sunday Club, Jeff was telling us about prayer. He said prayer is talking to God. We can ask him for anything we want and as long as it's a good thing, he will give it to us. No. He didn't quite say that. He said something like, "God will answer in the best possible way." Someone asked him what he meant and he said God doesn't do things the way we might expect him to.

For example, he said when we pray we might say, "Please, God, will you make the person who gets at me at school go to another school or pick on someone else instead of me" (though I don't think that second bit is a very nice thing to pray). We might think the best way out of the problem is for the bully to go somewhere else and leave us alone, but that's telling God how to sort out the problem. And he might have a different way – like making them be friends instead of enemies.

Winston made a rude noise. "I'd pray for them to get beaten up," he said. But that's Winston. Nobody really thought he meant it and Jeff didn't take any notice.

Anyway, the things Jeff said made me think about how Lottie and I could be friends again without her wanting me to stop being friends with Ruth. So I prayed about it. I couldn't think how God might do it, so I'll have to wait and see what happens.

I wonder if it will work – the prayer, I mean? And how long it might take. Jeff said God has a different timetable to us, so not to expect answers straight away. I think if Mum heard all this she'd say Jeff was making excuses for when prayers don't get answered.

〰〰〰〰〰〰

Dear Reader, as this book is supposed to be the story of my life I suppose I have to tell everything – well, not everything because there's lots of things that are too boring to talk about, like getting up in the morning, getting washed, having breakfast and so on and so on. Now I come to think about it, most of my life is spent doing the same thing over and over again – a bit like Mum's ironing and washing. Oh dear, that brings me back to what I'm now going to have to tell!

Mum and I have fallen out. It's a bit complicated. It's hard to know where to start. It wasn't really her fault but I don't think it was mine either.

It had to do with me needing a new pair of trainers. Everyone at school has got these really cool trainers, even Ruth. They cost a lot of money, about twice what you'd pay for ordinary ones. No, even more than that. I wouldn't have minded having just ordinary ones. Ruth only had ordinary ones until a few weeks back.

Then she had an auntie come to visit who earns pots of money in her job in America. They only see her once in a while. Ruth says she always brings lots of presents when she comes because she feels sorry for them. Ruth's mum doesn't work and Jeff doesn't earn a lot so they always get their clothes in charity shops – well, nearly always. I think she does have some new things, like underwear. But you can't see that, can you? So it doesn't count.

Anyway, Ruth's auntie brought stuff from America for the twins but she didn't know Ruth's size. So she took her to the West End – and invited me to come along, too. We had a fantastic time trying on loads of different things. At least, I had a fantastic time even though she wasn't buying anything for me. It didn't stop me trying things on, to keep Ruth company, and at least I was making the most of a day out.

I think Ruth was a bit embarrassed. She kept looking at the price labels and trying to find the cheapest things. So her auntie and I both ended up nagging her into choosing what she liked best. You wouldn't have had to nag me. I'd have gone wild if I had an auntie like Ruth's.

In the end Ruth found some really cool patterned jeans and a greeny coloured top to go with them that really suits her blonde hair. Then we had pizza and ice cream before walking back to the bus stop. On the way we passed this shoe shop with these fab trainers in the window. So we stopped and looked and drooled and before we knew it, we were inside the shop and Ruth was trying them on. She was scarlet in the face by the time we came out, with all her bags and the trainers. I was glad for Ruth, but I was also a bit mad at her for not being as over the moon as I would have been. I mean, I was just longing for a pair myself and wishing I had an auntie like hers with lots of money to spend on me. But, as Mum says, there's no pleasing some people.

So when Mum said she was getting me some trainers I begged and pleaded with her to get me some like Ruth's. She was going to until she found out how much they cost, and then she said no – she didn't slog her guts out over a hot iron so that I could pretend to be the daughter of a millionaire. Then she dragged me down to the market and bought some off a stall that looked like the real thing but weren't, and only someone like Mum wouldn't notice the difference.

I said I'd rather wear my old trainers till my toes came through, cos then people could feel sorry for me, instead of laughing at me. If even Ruth can get the real thing – and everyone knows she's poor – where does that leave me? We argued and shouted and other people who were there started on about how kids of today don't appreciate anything, and I wanted the ground to swallow me up.

I tried to make out that none of the trainers I tried on would fit me but Mum was so mad by this time that she bought my size anyway and said she didn't care if I got blisters up to my knees. And she threw my old ones away so I've got to wear the new ones anyway.

When I complained to Ruth, she said she wished her auntie hadn't spent all that money on her because there were so many poor kids in the world who hadn't got any shoes at all. Great, I thought. Cheer me up. But then she said we could swap if our feet were the same size, and they are! So we swapped and I was all cheerful. Ruth was happy enough, too. She likes being poor. I think it makes her feel good.

But Mum found out and made a big scene. She dragged me down to Ruth's and made me give them back, even though Ruth's mum didn't seem to mind all that much. Mum was mad because she said I'd shown her up, and made it look as though she didn't care about me. Anyway, it was horrible. And I hated her just then because she made it look as though I'd shown her up on purpose. All I wanted was a pair of trainers like everyone else. What's so bad about that? She just doesn't understand how important it is, especially when you get people like TB making fun of you – and Lottie.

Even Lottie's got designer trainers. She said she bought them with her own money. How come she has so much? She said she was buying them through her mum's catalogue instead of having pocket money and maybe my mum was too poor to give me pocket money, because all she did was other people's washing. She didn't have a proper job like her mum. I felt like hitting her but decided I'd ignore her instead, otherwise she'd think she'd scored one over me by being nasty about my mum.

I can't write any more. My hand aches and thinking about it all makes me feel both angry and sad at the same time.

Chapter eight

I'm supposed to be revising. We've got tests tomorrow but I can't think straight about anything. I don't even care if I do badly in the tests, I just feel so bad inside. You see, I haven't finished telling what happened, and I need to tell someone.

I can't tell Ruth because she'd tell me to tell God, and I don't know how to talk to God. I did try praying about Lottie, and where did that get me? Her being nasty about Mum. I don't know if that means God didn't hear me, or if prayer is a waste of time. But I know I can't talk to God, anyway, because of what I've done. I can only talk to you, dear Reader, and then make sure Mum doesn't find this book.

I didn't mean to do anything wrong. I was just trying to put things right with Mum. I thought I'd be really nice to her. Give her a big surprise.

She was granny-sitting for someone. She does that sometimes, when people go out and don't want to leave old people on their own – a bit like babies. It's easier than ironing and she can watch telly while she looks after them. They usually want to watch telly anyway, she says. She did moan a bit because Madame Stravinsky wants some special sewing done. She's been on a crash diet and her dresses are too big for her now. She wants Mum to take them all in and she wants them all NOW. As if she could wear them all in one day. But she's like that. Wants everything done yesterday. Mum says it's no wonder she's a nervous wreck.

Anyway, I thought I'd show Mum I was sorry – not about wanting the trainers but about what happened because of wanting them (I can't be sorry about wanting them when everyone else has them, can I?) – by doing some ironing for her while she was out, as a surprise.

I didn't think it would be very difficult – Mum makes it look easy. I've watched her hundreds of times so I know how she does it, and she's always saying she's got this special iron that knows as much about it as she does. I thought I'd only do easy things, like pillow cases and towels and little kids' stuff, and everything was going all right until I decided just to finish off Madame Stravinsky's bits and pieces, which Mum always washes by hand because they're so delicate.

She has such pretty things, soft and silky. Mum says she could buy a whole wardrobe with what Madame S spends on underwear. I remembered to switch to the right heat but as soon as I put the iron on the very first piece, something went badly wrong. It was a gorgeous creamy coloured slip and I could see the whole outline of the iron on it.

At first I thought it was going to be all right. The mark seemed to disappear, but when I picked it up to have a closer look, right under the light, there were little tiny holes in the material where the shape of the iron had been. I couldn't believe it. I don't know how it happened. It must have been the iron's fault, not mine.

It was like the end of the world. I felt sick. What would Mum say? She'd kill me. She'd never believe it was an accident. She might even think I'd done it on purpose, to get my own back over the trainers.

My mind went blank and all I could think of was throwing the slip away so Mum would never find out. I put it in a plastic bag and straight away took the rubbish downstairs to make sure Mum wouldn't accidentally come across it. Then I went to bed and when Mum came in I pretended to be asleep.

This morning she was pleased I'd emptied the rubbish, as well as doing some ironing for her. I was so scared, even though I knew she couldn't possibly know what had happened. Just as well Mum wasn't looking at me – she was making some toast. I rushed off as quick as I could, earlier than usual. I felt so bad, especially as Mum seemed to think that everything was now all right between us.

I had to wait for Ruth, because she wasn't quite ready. Her mum said a prayer for both of us before we left, something about having a good day and being kept from harm. If only she knew the harm that had been done already and I hadn't been kept from it! Just then I wanted to tell her what had happened. I was sure she'd understand, but something stopped me and I went to school wondering if God knew what I'd done and what he'd think of me.

I hoped everything would be OK, but when I got home from school the first thing Mum did was ask me about the missing slip. She'd taken the things back and – guess what – Madame S particularly wanted the one I'd ruined. It went with the dress she was planning to wear that day and she was absolutely certain it had been in the last lot of washing she'd given to Mum.

I said I didn't know anything about it, that I hadn't touched Madame S's things, I would have been too scared to. I couldn't tell what Mum was thinking. She looked kind of puzzled. Then I made the excuse about having to revise, and I'm stuck in my room, pretending to be working so Mum won't bother me, at least not till supper. Maybe by then she'll have forgotten.

Dear Reader, I am a prisoner! Except for going to the toilet, I can't leave my room and I'm to stay here until I sort myself out. (That's Mum's way of saying "until I confess and say sorry".) She says I can even eat in here because she doesn't want to be put off her food by the sight of me, so here I am. It's Friday night and I shall be stuck here till Monday morning – the whole weekend gone for ever!

If I had a mobile phone I could at least talk to Ruth but, to be honest, I don't want to talk to Ruth. I would have to tell her what happened.

She was expecting me to go down to her place this evening. She came up with this idea about us reading the Bible together and talking about it. It sounded fun because I haven't started reading the Bible they gave me for Christmas. I've only really looked at the pictures. It all looks so complicated. Ruth said it's easy when you know how, so I said, "Do you know how?" and she said, "Yes" and that's when she came up with this brill idea.

If Ruth knew what had happened, would she be on my side? Would she understand? Or would she be on Mum's side, blaming me for the mess I'm in? Ruth never seems to get herself into trouble. No wonder Lottie calls her a 'goody-goody'.

I really want to go down and start reading the Bible. But how can I ever get to know God if I keep doing things wrong? He won't want to listen to me, any more than Mum does.

Mum said what upset her most was that I told her lies. She said that really hurt her because it meant we weren't really friends. Friends don't lie to each other, she said. And I shouted back, "If we were friends, you'd believe me instead of that silly old Madame Stravinsky."

I was going to own up, but none of it happened the way I wanted it to. I had it all worked out in my mind. Because Mum didn't go on about it last night, I thought I'd wait and see what happened. If Mum found out, I'd explain and say I was sorry. (After all, if she didn't find out, there wouldn't be any point in saying anything, would there?) And it would all be calm and reasonable with a happy-ever-after ending.

But I forgot about one thing, didn't I? Our Irish tempers.

It's easy to write it down on paper, now I'm all calm. But Mum sort of grabbed me as I came in from school. She's not always home when I come in so I wasn't ready for her. I was thinking about going to Ruth's as soon as I'd had my supper and somehow I'd forgotten for a moment about the trouble I was in.

"Right, young Lucy Doherty, let's be having the truth now and no more nonsense!" were her first words and that made me see red.

Whenever Mum calls me "young Lucy Doherty" I know I'm in BIG trouble. There was real fury in her eyes. She'd been working up to it all afternoon, I bet. Maybe all day – just as soon as she found out from Madame S that the slip had been in the laundry bag.

So I shouted back and from then on it was just Mum and me screaming at one another, not even listening, and Mum saying thanks to me Madame S wouldn't trust her any more and she'd lose a lot of money and it was all my fault. And I was angry that Mum believed Madame S before she believed me.

So I still haven't told the truth. And until I do I'm grounded. I stormed into my room and wouldn't come out when Mum shouted at me to do so. So then she said I could stay here until it suited her, which wouldn't be until I told her what had happened to the slip. "That's all I'm asking you," she said. "What have you done with it?"

I was really stupid. I know that now. I should have told her but something bad in me wouldn't let me and now I don't know what to do. I haven't eaten my supper. I'm on hunger strike so the pizza and chips are staring at me from the plate on the floor. And I'm starving.

Name _____

Subject _____

Chapter nine

Another seven days of my life have gone by! When I last put pen to paper (that's the way some old-fashioned people talk about writing) I was in a state of great misery and anger. But right now I'm writing with a brand new fountain pen, a present from Mum. She had to get me a new pen for school but she could have got a cheapie. Instead, it's a Parker, and my favourite colour – purple. She didn't actually say it was to make up for being mean about the trainers. But she did say it was because she was sorry about calling me a liar.

Everything with Madame S has been sorted out and I'm no longer in the doghouse!

I should be over the moon, and I was at first, but now I feel bad about it again. I am fed up with myself. Sometimes I wish I didn't have feelings. They're such a nuisance. It's nice to feel happy but it's horrible feeling sad and even worse feeling angry. Why are there more bad feelings than good ones? And why can't I just have good feelings all the time?

As this is the story of my life, I must try to explain. I finished the last bit of my story with me being a lonely prisoner, cut off from friends and family, cut off from the whole world. And I was on hunger strike, too.

Luckily, I had a good book to read and I read and read and read until I finished it. That took me till about two in the morning and then I must have fallen asleep.

The next day was Saturday and Mum took back all the sewing she was going to do for Madame Stravinsky. That made Madame S so upset that she said maybe she did make a mistake after all. Maybe the slip wasn't in the last lot of laundry. And she gave Mum a big box of the yummiest chocolates I've ever eaten – from Harrods, no less – and so that afternoon we scoffed the lot between us.

By 'us' I mean me, Mum and Ruth because Mum came home and said I could come out of my room. (Actually, while she had been at Madame S's I had been out but I didn't tell her that.) She said she was sorry for not believing me but it was just that I looked so guilty and it was, after all, such a big coincidence – me doing the ironing that night and the slip disappearing. And then she gave me a hug and said I could invite Ruth up for the afternoon, seeing as she didn't let me go down to her the night before. I couldn't believe my ears – or my luck.

Mum gave me the money to hire a video and Ruth helped me choose it and we all sat on the settee with the chocs and had a brill afternoon. Mum was sewing at the same time, of course, but she's an expert at doing two things at once.

And I decided I would never make fun of Madame Stravinsky again. By being so dotty, she saved my life (well, almost), and made Mum believe me.

Mum was so nice to me all week that I really began to feel bad. But now I've cheered up because it was an accident, after all, and only because I'd wanted to do something nice for her. So I've put it all out of my mind, like Mum says – water under the bridge.

I wonder where all that water goes to?

I have this horrible feeling that God knows all about me because at Sunday Club today Jeff was talking about being sorry for the wrong things we do and SAYING sorry, too. I felt myself going all hot and I was terrified that everyone would see my face all red, so I pretended to have a cough. I coughed as hard as I could and covered my face with my hands, and then Jeff said I'd better go and get a drink of water.

There was no one in the kitchen so I stayed there for a while till I felt cool again. I didn't want to go back to the club room. I was scared about what else Jeff might say. I felt as if God knew exactly what had been going on, as if he could see right inside me and knew how bad I was. And suddenly I felt sorry for Madame S because, in the end, she had taken the blame for something I did wrong, and it wasn't fair. But how could I ever say sorry, and what was the point, anyway?

The next minute Vicky was there. She helps Jeff with the Sunday Club. She's nice and very pretty. She can play the guitar, too, but not like Jeff. I was really surprised to find out she's Winston's big sister. Winston is so awful but his sister is a real Christian, so Ruth says.

"Are you all right?" she said. "You've been here such a long time."

I nodded but she could see I was almost crying.

"Do you want to tell me what's up?" she asked.

I shook my head. "I just feel sick," I said, which was true.

Then she asked if I wanted her to pray for me. Vicky likes praying for people. I've seen her praying for grown-ups in the church. But I didn't want her to pray for me. I didn't want God anywhere near me just then. He could only be angry with me and that would make things worse. She could see I didn't want to talk, so she asked if I wanted to go back to Sunday Club or if I would rather go home. Ruth could go with me if I wanted.

I did want to go home, but I didn't want Ruth to go with me in case she started asking questions and going all holy on me. So I went back to Sunday Club with Vicky and pretended I was all right.

I got back at the worst part. Everyone had been given a piece of paper. Jeff said we could write on the paper anything we wanted to say sorry for. It would be like a prayer. If we wrote it down only God would see it. Jeff wasn't going to look. We could take it home and tear it up afterwards, or keep it if we wanted to remember our prayer.

Winston said he needed ten sheets of paper and Jeff took him seriously and counted out nine more. Everyone laughed but everyone started writing – everyone but me. I don't know what Winston was doing but at least he was putting something on the paper. I couldn't think of anything.

Well, that's not true. I was thinking all the time of YOU KNOW WHAT but I couldn't bring myself to write it down, even though it's all in my book.

Jeff suddenly said, "If it's too hard to write down, all you need to do is write the word 'sorry'. Jesus will know what you are sorry about."

I thought he could see me not knowing what to put. So I wrote SORRY in HUGE letters across the page. I did it slowly so Jeff would think I was writing something, but in my heart was something very hard and angry. And my throat was going all funny, like when you're going to cry. And I wished I'd never started coming to Sunday Club.

That doesn't make sense, of course, because it's only through Sunday Club that me and Ruth really became friends – though Sunday Club is also what made me and Lottie fall out. Why is life so complicated?

Dear Reader, I haven't written anything for ages. For one thing it's been that time of year – SATs and stuff – and I want to do well because it'll make a difference in my new school. I don't really want to write about school at all – after all, who wants to THINK about school once you get home, let alone WRITE about it? School is the least important thing in my life, even if it takes up most of the time (except sleeping, I suppose, but at least you can have fun dreaming so it's not wasted).

When I said that to my Mum (about school being the least important thing in my life) she put on the typical mother act instead of being my friend. She said she wished she'd done better at school but she hadn't had the chance and now never would and I mustn't make the same mistake. "You don't want to end up like me," she said, "feeding a washing machine all day long."

"I thought you were happy the way you are," I said.

"And so I am. But I could have been just as happy doing something else that wasn't such hard work."

"Didn't you bother to study?" I asked her.

"No. I just wanted to be free, so I dreamt the hours away instead of putting my mind to things."

I liked it when she said that, because I know what

she means. I sometimes dream the hours away. I can see Miss Brisbane in front of the blackboard yacking away and she seems to get smaller and smaller and her voice kind of disappears and then it's almost as if she's not there. I have to blink my eyes and shake my head to bring her back.

I wonder if she knows her nickname – Wallaby. We call her that because of her name. She's not really Australian but she does look a bit like a wallaby, small, with gingery hair, a long nose and sort of punchy hands that she waves about a lot. She's quite bouncy, too. Mostly, I like her. She says nice things about me to Mum on Parents Evenings and she knows I'm a dreamer.

"And where's Lucy Doherty this morning?" she'll suddenly shout out to bring me back to the real world, and everybody laughs.

But what is the real world? Who is the real me? That's the big question that's bothering me at the moment. Am I the person everyone can see on the outside – the one I can see in the mirror – or the one only I know about and no one else?

Before I started writing this evening I looked at myself in the mirror. I could see a face staring back at me. "That's Lucy Doherty," I imagined someone saying. "She's a pretty girl." "No, she's not. She's ugly," said another voice, and the next minute I was making up this imaginary conversation between two people who thought they knew me and were saying bad and good things about me.

I pulled all sorts of faces and made myself laugh, and then I just stared at myself and that scared me, because the more I stared the more I wondered who I was staring at.

Mum came into my room just then to remind me I hadn't done the washing up. Mum's reminders always mean DO IT NOW, so I did and I was happy to for once, cos sometimes it's nice just to chat to Mum instead of being on my own, thinking too much.

Mum says I'm growing up. After summer I'll be in Year 7 – secondary school. I've got to have a uniform. Everyone's been talking about Year 7 and wondering who's going to which school.

That's enough about school! There's another reason why I haven't written anything lately and that's because life is becoming more complicated all the time.

Falling out with Lottie was bad enough but now I'm scared I might be falling out with Ruth, too. If I do, it will be my fault because I've been making excuses for not seeing her in the evenings.

Mum joined this aerobics club and she said I could join, too. It's good fun and I like doing it but I mainly said yes because I wanted an excuse for not doing Bible reading with Ruth. I got scared about it. I thought if Ruth started asking lots of questions she'd find out what sort of person I really am and then she wouldn't like me any more.

It's funny. When you start thinking about God you kind of get this feeling that you have to be real – at least, that's how I feel, and when I'm pretending it makes me feel bad, as if he knows what I'm thinking, even though nobody else does.

I can't hide from him. He knows all about the lies I've told and the bad feelings I sometimes have. I wish I could do something about it – put things right somehow – but I can't ask Ruth without explaining things.

Mum wondered why I hadn't been down to Ruth's or invited her up here, and why I'd missed the last two Sunday Clubs. "What's happened?" she asked. "I hope you're not falling out with Ruth now as well as Lottie."

"Of course we haven't fallen out. Ruth's not like Lottie. We'll always be best friends."

"Well, I wish the two of you could be friends with Lottie. Why can't you make it up?"

"I would if she'd say sorry!" I burst out. "But she's so mean to Ruth and to me."

"Lottie was always a nice kid but she'll go wrong if nobody helps her. You ought to help. All this Christian stuff you and Ruth go on about. What good is it unless you put it into practice?"

"How do you mean?" I was getting so hot and uncomfortable and angry. Here I was, being blamed again – this time for something not my fault. It wasn't fair.

"Well, isn't Christianity supposed to be about turning the other cheek and forgiving your enemies? How long are you going to keep it up?"

"Oh, Mum, what do you know about it? If Lottie hangs around with the wrong sort of people it must be because that's the kind of people she really likes, the kind of person she really is, and that's not my fault or Ruth's."

And I stormed out.

"You should be ashamed of yourself, Lucy Doherty," she shouted through the door at me. I burst into tears but if she heard she didn't take any notice. I was glad really. She'd probably call me a drama queen and I hate it when she does that.

Name _____

Subject _____

Chapter ten

Something terrible has happened.

Greg is in hospital. We don't know if he's dead or dying. When I came home from school Mum told me he'd been rushed there this morning. He'd either taken an overdose or tried to kill himself. No one knows quite what happened and his mum hasn't come back from the hospital yet.

Everything has been so strange. I feel like we're living in a dream. The only way I can remember Greg is when he used to be so good-looking and both Lottie and I had a crush on him. I can't imagine him being dead, and yet when I think about the last time I saw him – so thin and dirty and desperate...

Lottie's mum came down to talk to my mum but they didn't talk very much really, except to say the same things over and over. Lottie came with her and somehow I was glad she was there. We didn't really look at each other but I could see she'd been crying, the same as I had.

And then the strangest thing happened. Our mums started praying. They seemed to know the same prayers and they went on and on for ages, just repeating things, and I wondered if God was listening or even if he was really there or, if he was, why did he let such a terrible thing happen to Greg? Why didn't he stop him doing whatever he did?

Lottie and I just sat there, staring at them, and I wished and wished we were still friends so we could talk about things. Our mums seemed to have forgotten about us.

If I'd been as brave as Ruth I might have said to Lottie, "Shall we pray, too?" but I still didn't really know how to talk to God and maybe Lottie didn't either. And I was scared she might laugh at me, or tell TB about it, and I was miserable for being such a coward.

But in my heart I was saying, "Please, God, don't let Greg die. Please make him better. You can do anything. Don't let him die." Maybe Lottie was doing the same.

I was really surprised at Mum.

It has been the strangest day of my life.

~~~~~~~

I think God does answer prayer but not in the way we expect. (I've just remembered that Jeff said that once and now I know it's true.) I can't remember all the things I've prayed about but all of a sudden things have happened, unexpected things. And all because Greg tried to kill himself.

My head is buzzing with all the things I want to write down and I can't write fast enough. This is the biggest thing that has happened in my life so far and the most important part of my book. Ruth wanted to come up this evening but I said I'd be too busy writing. She looked a bit surprised – she'd forgotten I'd told her ages ago that I'm writing a book. Or perhaps she didn't really believe it. Most people don't.

Mum has forgotten all about it. At least, she never asks about it now. I don't mind. I don't want her to read it – at least, not for years and years – not till I'm grown up. No one knows it's the story of my life. When Mum once asked I just said it was about a girl who had problems.

The most important thing is that me and Mum had

a BIG TALK! And I mean BIG, REALLY BIG! It was after Lottie and her mum went home. Mum went to the kitchen to start getting supper ready. I was absolutely bursting to know how she could sit and pray like that with Lottie's mum when she said she didn't believe in God. So I asked her. I just couldn't not ask, however mad it might make her. I just had to know. How did they know the same words?

Mum explained how she'd learned all those words when she was a kid in Ireland. She said they were special prayers that everyone in Ireland said and so she knew them by heart, the same as Lottie's mum. They had the same religion.

"But why did you pray if you don't believe in God?" I said.

"Because sometimes, m'darling, when things go wrong, when really bad things happen, that's all anyone can do. And who knows? Maybe there is a God somewhere and he'll have mercy on that poor boy and his mother."

"Does God listen to everybody's prayers then, even when you don't believe?" I asked.

"How should I know? But if you're drowning in a river you shout out for help even though you don't know if anyone's listening."

I asked her if she'd ever prayed before and if God had answered her prayers, and she said, "If he had answered, maybe I'd have more faith."

I can't remember everything we said while she was doing our supper, but somehow I found myself saying, "Mum, please tell me about Ireland, about your life there before you came here, what made you run away from home, why you never talk about things – about your parents – everything."

"It's water under the bridge," she started to say, but I burst in, "Mum, please. I want to know. If we were really best friends we wouldn't have any secrets. Please, please tell me. I'm old enough to know things. I'm not a little kid any more. You said so yourself. I'm growing up and I want to know."

For a while she didn't answer. She didn't even look at me and I was scared. I thought she was going to explode with anger (my mum does explode sometimes, just like a volcano). There was such a silence while she put sausages and chips and beans on our plates and then carried them to the table.

"Sit down," she said, and for a minute we concentrated on eating without looking at each other. I couldn't even taste the sausages (best Irish pork) but eating was better than doing nothing. And then she started talking – telling me everything I wanted to know, things I'd never imagined, things she'd kept secret for years.

It was such a sad story that soon I was crying. The tears just rolled down my cheeks and probably into my dinner. We both forgot about eating. We sat on the settee and Mum put her arms round me and went on talking and she told me the whole story.

Even thinking about it now makes me want to cry. I feel angry, too, angry that people can be so hard and cruel, and Mum said she never wanted to tell me because she didn't want me to be sad or feel sorry for her because she's happy the way she is and I'm the best thing that ever happened to her.

She let me ask her lots and lots of questions – all the questions I've always wanted to ask – even about my dad – and now I know everything. I'm not going to write it down now because it's late and

I'm tired – writing so much makes my wrist ache! But 'tomorrow is another day' (that's what Mum says when she tells me it's time to put the light out) and I've lots lots more to write.

We had a real cuddly time together like we haven't had for ages. Mum didn't even put the telly on or do any mending.

We just sat and talked like best friends do and I was so happy as well as so sad, and we both laughed and cried and hugged one another and it was one of the best days of my life.

THE STORY OF MY MUM

My mum was the youngest child of a family of six children. Of course she didn't know when she came into the world that she had three brothers and two sisters already. She was a little tiny baby and didn't know anything about anything. She didn't know that two days after she was born her mother died. Nor did she know that, because of what happened, her father didn't want her. He said he'd always be reminded that she'd killed her mother and he couldn't bear the sight of her.

She went to live with her grandmother. She was almost 60 years old and not very well, not well enough really to look after a baby. But she felt sorry for her, so she brought her up and called her Mary (her dad hadn't even bothered to think of a name for her). The rest of the family hardly knew her. All they knew was what their dad had told them – that it was Mary's fault their mother had died, so they didn't love her very much. They hardly ever saw her even though they lived in the same town.

She was happy with her gran but by the time she was five Gran couldn't cope any more and had to stop looking after her. Her dad still didn't want her. He'd married again and had two more children and everybody seemed to have forgotten about her so she was put in a home. Gran visited her from time to time but then she died and Mary had no one left in the world who cared about her at all. She was only seven years old.

When she left the home she had nowhere to go, so her dad said she could live with him. She was all excited about that, thinking that perhaps at last he'd forgiven her for what she'd done to her mother by being born. But all he really wanted was someone to look after him because his new wife had left him and he was all on his own. (Her brothers and sisters had all grown up and got married and didn't want to know. He was not a nice man so nobody wanted to stay with him.)

My mum thought this was her chance to really get to know her dad. Even though he'd been so mean to her she hoped that if she was kind to him and looked after him, he'd forgive her and love her. So she tried and tried for years. She said all she wanted was for him to call her his daughter and show that he didn't blame her any more for what had happened so long ago. And she pretended to herself that one day it would happen. He'd talk to her about it and say sorry.

She used to dream about that day. That's all that kept her going. She so badly wanted him to love her because there was nobody else. She did everything she could to please him but then she realised that he was just taking advantage of her. He didn't care about anybody but himself.

She tried to get to know her brothers and sisters but it was a waste of time. She was like a stranger to them as their dad had made them hate her. And anyway, they all had their own lives, and weren't interested.

They told her not to bother with him but to go and make her own life somewhere, as far away as possible.

"They just shut the door in my face," she said. "Every one of them."

She'd gone with flowers or a box of chocolates or little things for their kids. But most of all she'd gone with a heart longing to be loved by someone – her own flesh and blood. But they didn't have any love to spare and she felt like the loneliest person in the world.

She never told anybody how she felt. She was too ashamed so she pretended it didn't matter and was as cheerful as anyone could be, always singing and dancing and having fun and making people laugh. And then she met my dad and everything changed. She fell madly in love with him and for the first time in her life she had someone who really cared about her (Gran had cared but she could hardly remember her).

Her dad wasn't pleased at all. He wanted to keep her at home and didn't like the idea he'd be on his own again one day if she married him. He kept saying nasty things about him but she didn't care, she was so happy. At long last everything was going to be all right.

But it wasn't. Everything fell apart when she found out she was pregnant with me. She told my dad and asked him how soon they could get married. And then he told her he was married already and had a little girl. She didn't even know but she did know that he loved her.

"It was one of those things that happen," she said. "You mustn't go blaming him. He never wanted to hurt me. He never wanted to hurt them but he didn't know how to sort it out. So I had to sort it out for him."

That was the very worst time of her life. She said she wished she'd never been born. All she wanted was a bit of love, like other people had, but somehow it always went wrong.

She decided she'd come to England where no one she knew could find her. She couldn't bear the thought of that little girl (my half-sister) having her life messed up, as hers had been. She didn't want to hurt anyone and she wanted to start all over again.

"I had you," she told me. "You're all I want. I didn't want to risk any harm coming to you because you're the most important thing in the world to me, m'darling."

"More than my dad?" I asked, because she'd said how much she loved him, even though she never talked about him.

"Much more. You see, he's not mine to have, but you are."

"Did you never write to him? Does he know about me?"

She shook her head. "It would have been so difficult if we had kept in touch. I had to make a clean break and just put him out of my mind. Water under the bridge."

And that's when I told her how much I wanted to know my dad, how I was always thinking about him. And she hugged me tight and said she was sorry but she'd tried to do what was best – best for all of us.

She did tell me his name but I'm not going to write it down. It's our secret, Mum's and mine. But I can't help hating my grandfather and all his children, my aunts and uncles, because they couldn't love my mum even just a little bit, though none of it was her fault.

Name

Subject

Chapter eleven

I feel very strange, as if somehow I wasn't me. I can't explain it. I know all about my mum's family – my family – now, and apart from Gran (my great-grandmother) none of them seem very nice. Grandad is horrible. And all those aunts and uncles. They don't know about me. They don't know I exist and probably never will.

The strangest bit is my dad not knowing anything about me. I wonder if he's even forgotten that somewhere in the world he has a child? (He can't know whether I'm a boy or a girl. Does he ever wonder?) Has he ever wanted to know me like I've always wanted to know him? I wonder if he's forgotten my mum. She hasn't forgotten him. I could tell by the look in her eyes when she told me about him that she still loves him. That must be why she's never had another boyfriend.

It's really weird to suddenly discover things you've always wanted to know and then have them make you feel so different. I can't play my favourite pretend game any more about my dad coming round on a Saturday and asking me where I'd like to go because now I know he never will come.

And I don't dare ask my mum what he looks like, not because I don't think she'd tell me but because I want to keep thinking of him the way I always have, with black curls and twinkling eyes, like the man at the corner shop.

Somehow I feel kind of lost, as if I haven't got a dad any more. And that's silly because I've never had a dad, not like Ruth has, anyway. Before, he was there, somehow, belonging to me. But now I know he belongs to some other girl, older than me. And suddenly I feel like an orphan.

I know that's stupid. I've got the best mum in the world and she'll always love me better than anyone else. But – oh, I'm not going to write any more. It's all too complicated. Goodnight, dear Reader. I'm too tired to think.

Greg is alive! He's still in hospital. They are doing all sorts of things to him to get him better. He's hurting really badly but he's alive and that's what matters most. It's almost two weeks since he tried to kill himself and all sorts of things have happened since then, things that have never happened before.

For instance, all our mums seem to have got very chatty (mine, Ruth's and Lottie's I mean). My mum and Lottie's were always friends but I never knew Ruth's mum was friends with Lottie's. And I never knew how many people in the flats really cared about Greg and his mum.

Ruth's home is like a railway station – people coming and going, wanting to hear the latest news about Greg. He's not allowed ordinary visitors yet but the whole block is buzzing. (Mum would say I'm exaggerating. I suppose it's not the whole block but it seems like it. Lots of people, anyway. Whenever I go down to Ruth's there always seems to be someone there, asking about Greg.)

Lottie's nearly always there, too, looking after the twins. They absolutely adore her, so Ruth comes up to my place. She and her mum have arguments about the twins because she never wants to look after them when her mum's busy, especially if I'm there. She says they're a pain, always messing up her things, and they don't do what she tells them anyway. I think she's a bit jealous about the twins liking Lottie so much so I told her I think it's a plot to keep Lottie out of trouble – looking after them instead of going around with TB's gang. I didn't tell her what my mum had said about *us* helping her if we were real Christians.

Now I've written that, I've suddenly remembered how I once got angry with Ruth when she wanted us to try to make friends with Lottie again. I wonder if we could be friends? Lottie hasn't been so nasty to us at school since she's been looking after the twins. She talks a lot to Ruth's mum. Wouldn't it be funny if she started coming to Sunday Club? I bet she'd really like it if she did.

We've been praying for Greg in church and in Sunday Club and Greg's mum has been coming to church. She never used to but since Ruth's mum and dad have been helping her she's changed her mind. Ruth says she's sure it's only because people have been praying so much that Greg is still alive.

I'm beginning to think that prayer DOES work in a funny kind of way, not the way we expect. I always thought if you asked God for something he'd give it – just like that – like waving a magic wand and then everything being just the way you want it to be.

Now I'm starting to see that God's way of doing things is much more complicated and that's why we have to wait for things to happen. I can't really explain it but it really makes me want to talk to God a lot more (that's what prayer is, Jeff says, just telling him about your problems and things).

But some things you just can't talk about – like my

dad. It's all confused in my heart. Perhaps I don't need to SAY anything to God. Perhaps he just knows and will somehow sort it out. I really hope so because, although I'm glad about Greg, inside I feel really sad and strange. I want something to happen to me, deep inside, but I don't know what it is.

~~~~~~~~~~

Something HAS happened! I was feeling so miserable yesterday that I didn't want to go down to Ruth's or have her up here. I pretended to Mum I was going out but I just went for a walk round the block and then came back and sat on the stairs for ages, thinking about my dad and my half-sister and not knowing whether I hated them or was jealous or what.

Part of me wanted to go and tell Ruth all about it but another part didn't. It's funny about Ruth. She's my best friend but I can't share everything with her the way I used to with Lottie. Maybe it's because she's so serious. I'm glad she's my friend and I know she'd never let me down, but how can she understand about me and my dad? She's got such a great dad and she's always had him. And when she sometimes goes on about God and Jesus I feel kind of left out because she's always had them and I haven't.

Anyway, I was sitting on the stairs feeling really miserable, wishing Mum had never told me anything – even that she'd made up a story, like my dad being in prison on false charges, or being lost at sea – something romantic like in stories. And I was beginning to think about what could have happened to him if this was just a made-up story I'm writing – when suddenly Lottie was right in front of me.

She must have been coming up from looking after the twins, but I didn't hear her till she was there, her at the bottom of the stairs, me at the top. She stared at me and I could see she didn't know what to do. Maybe she thought I wasn't going to let her go by. She looked kind of confused. And all of a sudden I just burst into tears.

The next thing I knew Lottie was sitting on the stairs beside me, like we used to when we were friends, and then she started crying too. It was really weird, the two of us sitting there side by side, sobbing our hearts out without saying anything. She didn't know why I was crying and I didn't know why she was crying but somehow it made me feel good having her crying beside me.

By the time we stopped crying we both knew we were friends again. We didn't say anything but we knew. And then I started telling Lottie all about my dad. It just poured out of me, all the things I didn't have words for, all the things I couldn't say to my mum or Ruth, and I knew Lottie would understand. Although they'd all been glad when he went away, Lottie had once told me how she wished her dad hadn't been so bad because she really wanted to love him and have him love her.

We sat and talked about our dads for ages and it was like we'd never stopped being friends. Lottie said she absolutely hated Tracey Bignall and her crowd and she was really glad TB wasn't going to be in the same school with us next year. And she told me how miserable she'd been and how she'd never wanted not to be my friend.

And I said the same to her and Lottie laughed and said we'd been stupid and should be friends for ever.

"What about Ruth?" I asked. I had to be honest because I couldn't stop being friends with Ruth. I didn't want to.

Lottie was quiet for a minute. Then she said, "As long as Ruth doesn't mind about me I won't mind about her."

We would have jabbered on for ages longer but Lottie's mum stuck her head out of the door, wondering where she was, I expect. She looked surprised when she saw us together but all she said was, "Supper's ready," so Lottie went home after promising she wouldn't breathe a word to anyone about what I'd told her and we both knew it was all right.

I just feel so happy now. It's amazing. And I want to end this bit of my story by saying, "Thank you, God. You really are the bee's knees." (Can you say that to God? I hope so.)

Name

Subject

Chapter twelve

Dear Reader, it's been a few weeks since I wrote anything. Lots of things have been happening, which is just as well, otherwise the story of my life would be quite boring. As I don't know which of the things is the MOST IMPORTANT I think I'll just have to tell you about all of them and you can decide for yourself.

First of all – me, Lottie and Ruth. Will you believe it if I tell you that we're all best friends now? I can hardly believe it myself. In half-term holiday we spent just about every day together. We had picnics in the park (the first time our mums have let us go on our own – they've decided we're big and sensible enough at last); and we went to the library nearly every afternoon because they had a 'Tell us about a Book' week, which was fun.

We had to tell people about our favourite book – or the one we hated most – and why, and we could write book reviews and have them pinned up for everyone to see and read. I told people I was writing a book myself but then I wished I hadn't because the librarian wanted to know what it was about. I just said it was my autobiography.

She said, would I like to bring it to the next session and read bits of it, but I said no. It was private until it was published. She found me a book which tells you how to get a book published so I've been reading that instead of writing.

Ruth did a book review on the Bible. I thought it was very brave of her because the librarian looked a bit surprised (not nice surprised). Even Lottie thought she was brave AND said so. Ruth turned as red as a beetroot like she always does when she suddenly becomes the centre of attention, but

I think she was pleased.

Lottie hasn't started coming to Sunday Club yet but she's stopped going around with TB's gang and has been getting picked on by them. The Kellys have threatened to beat her up but we've promised to stay with her all the time and Ruth said she'd pray every night that Jesus would keep her safe. I said I'd do the same (but I don't always remember). Anyhow, Ruth must be remembering because so far we haven't seen the Kelly boys for ages and even TB seems to be leaving her alone, apart from the occasional nasty remark.

TB is getting more in with the crowd who are going to the local secondary school (not very nice). Our mums don't want us to go there. What a relief. We'll have to get a bus to our new school but at least we'll be going together and that will be fun. And we're going together with our three mums to buy our uniforms – red and grey (good colours for me and Lottie but not so good for poor Ruth).

One of the best days of the holiday was when we had a big FAMILY picnic. Ruth's parents organised it. Loads of people came. All Lottie's family as well as all Ruth's. Greg came with his mum. He was looking very wan (I found that word in the dictionary. It exactly describes just how Greg looked so if you want to know you'll have to look it up for yourself) but he's completely off drugs and getting better every day. His mum looks different too. She was laughing and smiling and talking to everybody.

There were some people from the church and – guess what – even my mum came! She actually left her laundry basket and her ironing board and Madame S's last-minute repairs and spent hours and hours in the park. I've hardly ever seen my mum enjoying herself so much.

The sun shone! It was HOT. The paddling pool was open so we splashed about a bit and between us all we bought nearly every ice cream from the van when it came round. (That's what it seemed like, anyway. It took the man ages to serve us all, especially when people kept changing their minds about what they wanted.)

Jeff organised some games for the little ones and he brought his guitar, so when we got tired of games and stuff he started singing. They were all songs about Jesus but everybody listened and some of the grown-ups joined in. He played an Irish tune that my mum knew – Danny Boy – so she sang HER words while Jeff sang his. Everybody clapped my mum when she finished and she looked quite pleased. It was one of the most special days I can remember.

∿∿∿∿∿∿∿

Last Sunday was the bestest day ever at church. (I don't think 'bestest' is a proper word, but it's all I can think of for the moment to describe something that's BETTER than best.)

Actually, dear Reader, I stopped at that point as I'd just remembered the thesaurus I bought last week. It's a very useful book for authors, one of our 'tools'. That's how the library book about writing describes it. Mum thought I was mad when I told her I was going to buy it (as I'm supposed to be saving some of my pocket money for holidays).

"How can I be a proper author without it?" I exclaimed. (That's another word for 'said'. There are hundreds in the thesaurus.)

As she couldn't answer that question, she said OK. So last Saturday me, Lottie and Ruth got a bus down to the shopping centre where there's a big bookshop that sells just about every kind of book you can imagine. I felt really excited and I think even Lottie and Ruth were impressed when they saw how big it was and how much it cost. They now know I'm really serious about being a writer and they keep asking me about THIS book.

So I'd better finish it as soon as I can. I still don't know if I'll let them read it. I might read out bits to them but not before I've put the final full stop. (That sounds good – 'The Final Full Stop'. It might be the title of my next book.)

"Lucy Doherty, you're getting carried away!"

I've just told myself that, because all I was going to write was a list of words from the thesaurus which mean 'bestest' – so here goes: bonzer (not heard that one before – I bet Lottie will like it); second to none; supreme; unparalleled; capital. Actually, I haven't copied them all – there's too many – so I've only chosen the ones that describe last Sunday best.

Last of all it says important, and I suppose last Sunday was important – important and special and... BONZER! (My favourite from now on.)

Anyway, back to last Sunday. It was special because Greg was going to be baptised. Yes – Greg! I couldn't believe my ears when I first heard about it. I thought only babies got baptised but Jeff told us all about it the week before in Sunday Club so that we'd understand what was happening.

He said when a person becomes a true believer in Jesus they have to be baptised. It's a sign that all the bad things they've ever done have been washed away. And it's a bit like a burial, too (like when we buried Chico). The bad old Greg is dead and buried. The new Greg has been born (I think that's how Jeff described it).

Winston, who just has to be clever, said, "Why don't they bury him properly in the ground?" Jeff always pretends to take Winston seriously and said back, "Why do you think?" so Winston looked a bit silly and shut up.

I must say I went home thinking I like the idea of being baptised. It's like starting again and showing everyone you're starting again so people can forget what you used to be like and just see the new you. "That's what God does," said Jeff. "He sees a new person."

And Greg is a new person.

It's hard to write about what happened last Sunday. I didn't know what to expect and the thing that surprised me most of all was how many people were there. The church was nearly packed out. There were loads of people I've never seen before and, dear Reader, you'll never believe this but it's absolutely true...

...MY MUM WAS THERE AND SO WAS ALL LOTTIE'S FAMILY!

I think everyone from the flats that knows Greg and his mum was there. We didn't have Sunday Club that day because it was a special service. And I was pleased because it meant I could stay sitting with Mum and Lottie and Ruth for the whole time.

I can hardly describe how it felt, having Mum there. I never thought she'd come though I gave her the special printed invitation and prayed and prayed beforehand that she'd say yes. Ruth and I prayed for Lottie and her family to come as well as my mum, and it worked because they did come and didn't make a fuss about it.

Mum said she was only coming because she wanted to support Greg and his mum (Lottie's mum said the same thing) but I was thrilled to bits anyway because I thought maybe Lottie would start coming to Sunday Club with me and Ruth. And guess what, even Madame S was there! Mum must have told her about it. She was dressed up to the nines and wearing the most extravagant hat you can imagine. Everybody stared at her, which is probably what she wanted anyway, so she was satisfied.

I think I'm kind of putting off getting to the most important part of the service because it was so weird and special and somehow scary (scary in a good way not a bad one) and hard to write about. We started off in the usual way, with a hymn, then the vicar explained what would be happening and said how most of us there either knew Greg or knew what had been happening to him but that Greg himself was going to tell us all about it.

So Greg stood up. He was still looking wan (I love that word!) but at the same time there was something different about him, something that made my heart start to thump – a bit like it used to when me and Lottie were in love with him.

And then he talked. He talked about how he'd got into drugs and all the bad things he'd done. And when he couldn't bear it any longer how he'd tried to kill himself. And even that didn't work. And he described the awful things the doctors had to do to him to save his life, and how he kept on wishing he could die because it was all so painful.

And then he started talking about Jesus, that somehow he knew Jesus was in the room with him all the time, not saying or doing anything but just being there, and how he knew he wasn't going to die because Jesus was there, and that everything was going to be different when he got better.

By this time just about everyone in church was crying. Greg was crying, too. The tears were running down his cheeks and he kept wiping his nose on his sleeve like a little kid. But it was a good kind of crying, as if all the hurting was being washed out of him.

I was crying, too, that's how I know it was a good sort of crying. It sounds weird but it was almost as if we were all crying for joy even though it hurt. And for the very first time I really felt as though Jesus was inside me – the same as he's inside Ruth and other real Christians. It was like he was in the church with us. I know he's always supposed to be there but last Sunday, for the first time, I knew it was true.

My heart was still thumping but it was because of Jesus, not Greg.

Everything was special about that day but the bit about Jesus and me was the most special bit of all, even though I can't explain it and haven't got words to write it down.

Dear Reader, we break up from school next Friday and we're having a school leavers' disco to celebrate. It's going to be quite a sad time. Funny. I've never felt sad about breaking up before. Some teachers I shall be glad never to see again but I shall miss Wallaby. She's about the only one who really understands me.

The following weekend I'm going on holiday with Ruth, to her auntie in Hastings by the sea. Mum's buying me a new swimsuit and lots of sun cream just in case we get some summer. I'm having a holiday with Lottie and her mum too! You'll never guess where! We're going to Italy to see Lottie's grandparents. There will be some sun there!

Franco and Tony are staying here with Ruth's parents. My mum's promised to help keep an eye on them, too. They're booked into a football club so they don't mind about not going to Italy. I've borrowed a phrase book from the library and me and Lottie are learning how to say hello and goodbye and "Can you tell me the way to the shops?" Lottie's accent is better than mine, probably because she's half Italian anyway. But she doesn't know any more than I do because her mum doesn't either.

There's no Sunday Club now till September so it's just as well we're going to have other things to do. There's a holiday club for a whole week and Lottie is coming to that. Hooray! I told her what happened to me at the special service. She was interested but said she didn't feel like that at all. She cried for Greg because he was crying but it hadn't made her think much about Jesus. I just hope the holiday club will make her feel different because there's lots of things about Jesus I want to share with her but right now I can't because she doesn't understand.

Ruth was over the moon when I told her what had happened and said we had to tell her parents. So we did and they both gave me a hug and said now I belonged to Jesus the same as they did. It made me feel really good inside. But there's still some things I've got to sort out. I haven't yet told my Mum the truth about Madame S's underwear. I go all cold inside just thinking about it, especially when it's all water under the bridge by now.

I've told Ruth and she says I must tell my mum.

"I think I'll wait till I come back from holiday in case she grounds me. She won't stop me going to Italy because I've already got the ticket but she could stop me going to Hastings," I said to Ruth, because she wanted me to tell her straight away.

But the look on Ruth's face made me think that I'll just have to tell her somehow before I go, otherwise I'm not going to enjoy myself.

"Jesus will give you the right words and if she does ground you then you'll still feel good about having told the truth," was the way she reasoned.

If she weren't my best friend I might think she didn't really care about me going on holiday with her. But she said she'd pray for it to be all right. All I need now is the courage – and the right moment – to spill the beans.

Anyway, dear Reader, you can see that I'm going to be so busy this summer, as well as having lots to think about and sort out, that I won't have time to do any writing at all. So this is where my autobiography is going to end for now. Perhaps next winter I'll start on part two but I really am looking forward to the final full stop. So here it comes –   .

If you've enjoyed this book, why not look out for another *Snapshots* title?

Different Shoes
Carol Hathorne

Gina would love to be a footballer – a real pro. But a terrible car accident means that she might never be able to play again. Will she have to give up her dreams, or does God have something new round the corner?

ISBN 1 85999 677 9

You can buy this book at your local Christian bookshop, or online at
www.scriptureunion.org.uk/publishing
or call Mail Order direct
01908 856006